Luke Temple was born on Halloween, 1988. As a child, Luke didn't enjoy reading and found writing  hard work. Yet today he's an author! When not writing, Luke spends most of his time visiting schools and bringing his stories to life with the children he meets.

LUKe'S bOOKS FOr 5-7 yeAr OLdS

Albert and the Blubber Monster

Albert and the Giant Squid

The Poo Monster

The Blubber Monster's Crown

LUKe'S bOOKS FOr 7-11 yeAr OLdS

'Felix Dashwood' books:

Traitor's Treasure

Mutating Mansion

Traitor's Revenge

'Ghost Island' books:

Ghost Post

Doorway To Danger

The Ghost Lord Returns

Short story book: *Zombie Cows from Outer Space*

 Find out more at:

WWW.LUKeteMPLe.co.UK

ALBERT AND THE
GIANT SQUID

Hi Bonnie!

Luke [signature] *2024*

LUKE TEMPLE
ILLUSTRATED BY JESSICA CHIBA

Gull Rock Publications

Dedicated to Peter Littlewood,
whose spooky campfire tales live with me still!

With special thanks to Mike Temple for the games, and with thanks
to Jessica Chiba, Catherine Coe, Gareth Collinson, Kieran Burling,
Jayne Grainge and Barbara Temple

WWW.LUKeteMPLe.co.UK

Copyright © Luke Temple 2015/2018/2022
Cover and illustrations © Jessica Chiba 2015
Blubber Monster illustration © Grace Ji 2022

First published in Great Britain by Gull Rock Publications

The paper used in the printing of this book has been made from wood grown in managed, sustainable forests.

ISBN: 978-0-9572952-6-1

Printed and bound by Clays Ltd, Elcograf S.p.A.

A catalogue record of this book is available from the British Library

Chapter One:

The Ship in the Sheep Field

The wind swept through Albert's hair as he rowed his small boat along the coast. His best friend, Ernie, lived on a farm at the north end of Thistlewick Island. It was Ernie's turn to feed the sheep that morning and Albert was going to help.

He arrived at a beach and dragged the boat onto the smooth, golden sand.

"Albie!" He looked up and saw his friend calling to him from the top of the cliff. "Something's happened!"

Albert wasn't sure if it was a good or a bad something. "Coming!"

He quickly climbed up the steep path to the top of the cliff and saw what Ernie meant. His mouth dropped open.

"Wow! That's huge!"

Sitting near the cliff edge was a ship, a hundred times bigger than Albert's boat. Its two masts towered into the sky.

Baaah!

The sheep were all staring at it from the other side of the field.

"How did it get up here?" asked Albert.

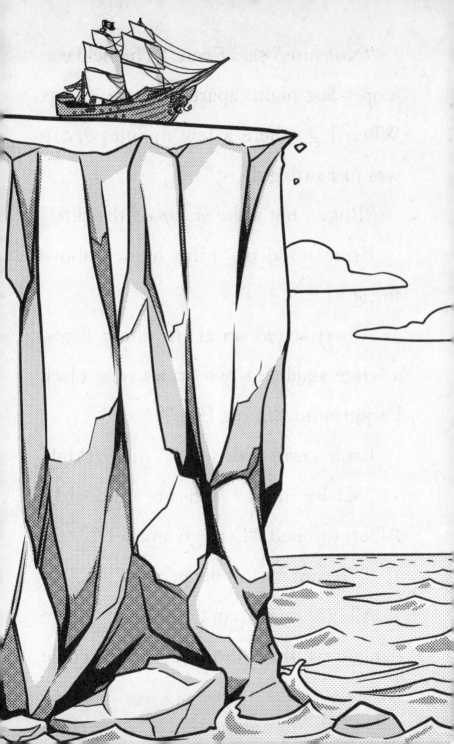

"Not sure," said Ernie. "The field was empty last night, apart from the sheep. When I got here a few minutes ago it was just sitting there."

"But … but we're *on top* of the cliff!"

Ernie nodded. "Fifty metres above the sea."

Albert stared up at the ship's flag – a white skull and two bones on a black background. "Look, Ern."

Ernie's eyes widened. "A pirate ship!"

"Maybe there's treasure onboard." Albert grinned. "Let's go and see!"

"No way, it's too dangerous."

Albert raised an eyebrow. "More dangerous than those evil merpeople who crashed our boat into the rocks last year?"

"Elody saved us that time."

Elody was a kind mermaid who had scared away the other merpeople and saved Albert and Ernie from drowning.

"She can't save us on top of a cliff," Ernie pointed out.

Albert shrugged and walked over to the ship to get a closer look.

"Be careful, Albie!"

Baaah!

Even the sheep were warning him. He ignored them and found a hole ripped into the side of the ship. Albert poked his head in. He didn't hear a single sound.

Baaah!

(Except for the sheep...)

"There's no one inside. We'll be fine. If you come in with me, I'll let you look after my special shell."

"The silver one Elody gave you?"

Albert nodded. Ernie was always asking if he could look at it.

Ernie bit his lip.

"OK."

He clenched his fists and stepped towards the ship.

Albert climbed in through the hole. The ship smelt stale and seaweedy. He grabbed Ernie's hands and helped him clamber in too.

Inside it was pitch black. Albert could only just make out the whites of Ernie's wide eyes.

"Let's see what we can find." Albert's voice bounced around the ship.

His heart started beating faster. Was it because he was excited or nervous?

He moved ahead slowly, waving his hands in front of him. Ernie brushed his arm.

"What's the matter?"

There was no reply.

"Where are you, Ern?"

He waited. Still no reply.

Albert's heart was thudding like a drum now.

"Ern?"

Baaah! replied a sheep from outside.

"*AAAHHHHH!*" came a bone-chilling cry.

Albert's heart stopped. "Ernie!"

Chapter Two:
The Inkhunter

Albert spun around. Why had Ernie screamed? Where was he? Albert felt around desperately for his friend. His left hand touched something metal. A door handle. He turned it and the door creaked open.

"Ern, are you in here?"

He stumbled forwards in the dark and his right foot landed in thin air.

"Woah!"

Albert tripped and tumbled downwards head first, and landed

with a thud on the hard floor. He sat up and rubbed his head.

Steps! he realised. *I've fallen down to the bottom of the ship.*

"Albie? Is that you?" came a small voice.

"Ern! Where are you?"

Suddenly bright light filled Albert's eyes. He squinted and saw Ernie in front of him, behind some thick iron bars.

"How did you get in there?"

"Run, Albie, j-just *run*!"

Albert frowned. What was making Ernie so frightened?

He felt something sharp at his neck and froze.

"You ain't going nowhere, sunshine," spat a gruff voice.

Shaking, Albert reached up and felt the cold point of a sword.

"*YAAAAARRR!*"

Out of nowhere five … eight … ten men appeared, all waving swords. The men were huge, with ripped clothes and scars on their faces. Pirates!

Albert gritted his teeth and looked up at the pirate holding a sword to his neck. Manky hair hung from a square head and an eye patch covered one eye.

"Stand up straight for Captain Fangarm!" the pirate ordered.

Cold sweat ran down Albert's face. These pirates were bad enough – what would Captain Fangarm be like?

A small person in a green jacket

stepped through the crowd. Many
dreadlocks sprung out from under a
wide-brimmed hat. Albert made out the
face of a woman. Her left hand shone

in the light
— no, not
her hand,
but a
silver
spike,
curved
and
sharp.

"Well, well, well, boys, welcome to my ship, the *Inkhunter*!" Despite her words, she didn't sound friendly. She sounded like a dog about to attack.

"*YAAAAARRR!*" came the pirates' cheers.

"Ernie's dad is just outside the ship," said Albert.

"Do not lie!" Captain Fangarm snarled, pointing her silver spike at him. "You are on your own."

Albert stared around. Every possible exit was blocked by pirates. He looked to Ernie, who was clinging to the bars of his cell.

"How ... how did you get the *Inkhunter*

into this field?" asked Albert.

"Well, that is quite a story. Should I tell him, lads?"

"YAAAAARRR!"

Chapter Three:
Captain Fangarm's Story

We had just won a fierce battle against another pirate ship, the *Crackletrap*.

My crew were all hungry, but no one was hungrier than me. I felt a rumbling in my stomach that only my favourite thing could satisfy: squid!

We had heard of a good spot to catch squid, just off Thistlewick Island. So we sailed here and Rocco, our cook, spent all of yesterday with his net in the water.

My hunger grew and grew, but there

was no sign of what I most desired.

"Where is all the squid?" I asked Rocco.

He just shrugged.

"You will stay up here and catch me a squid, or you will walk the plank!"

I returned to my cabin while the rest of the crew played cards and drank rum. I snoozed in my hammock, dreaming of the amazing taste of fresh slimy squid tentacle.

Then...

"AAAAARRRGGGHHH!"

... a scream woke me.

I leapt up, sword at the ready. "Who was that? Are we under attack?"

"It's Rocco, up on deck," Smullet replied.

I ran into the corridor and called, "What are you waiting for? Get up there! All of you! No one attacks my ship and gets away with it!"

The *Inkhunter* shook violently, throwing me and my pirates to the floor.

I tried to stand up but the ship

lurched
forwards
and I
slammed
into a
wall.

"What is causing this?" Smullet asked.

"We're cursed!" Hangma whispered.

"We're going to die."

"AAAAARRRGGGHHH!"

It was Rocco again.

The *Inkhunter* swung sideways and we all flew against the ceiling.

A rumbling, roa**aaar**ing sound started. The ship began flinging about, as if it had been tossed in the air.

THUD!

We landed heavily. The ship was now deadly still.

I rubbed my head, stood up and staggered over to a porthole.

"We're on land!" I realised. "The *Inkhunter* is on top of a cliff!"

Chapter Four:
Rocco

Albert realised his mouth was hanging open again. "So what made the *Inkhunter* fly up here?"

"Must have been the same thing that made Rocco scream," Captain Fangarm replied.

"W-what made him scream?" asked Ernie.

"We don't know. The thing is, we've never heard Rocco say a word. He's meant to be mute. That's why I was so surprised to hear him scream. There he is. Rocco!" she called.

The pirates parted to let a man through, dressed in rags like the rest of them, but hunched over and shaking. His arms were wrapped tightly around a glass bowl, with many pink tentacles floating inside it.

"Is that a squid?" asked Albert.

"Yes. Rocco caught it before he screamed. Doesn't it look delicious?"

"Um … I guess?" Albert didn't dare say what he really thought — that it looked like the last thing he'd want to eat.

"If only I could get it off him!" the captain barked.

Her eyes flashed wide open with greed. She moved towards Rocco but the pirate jabbed his sword around, one arm clutching the bowl tighter.

"And we can't catch any more squid because my ship is stuck up here!" Captain Fangarm turned to Smullet. "I've had enough. Lock this boy up with the other one."

Smullet grabbed hold of Albert's collar and lifted

him off the ground. Albert looked to Ernie, who stared helplessly back from behind the bars. Albert had to think of something to save his friend – and himself.

"Wait!" he cried, dangling in mid-air. "I'll find a way to get your ship off this cliff."

"What?" Captain Fangarm spat.

Smullet lowered Albert and the pirates glared at him. He shrunk down, certain the captain was about to attack him with her spike.

"Alright," she said slowly. "Much better that a runt like you tries to do it. If anything bad happens to you, that's no skin off my teeth."

"*YAAARRR!*" the pirates cheered in agreement.

Albert stuck out his chest, doing his best to look confident. "But I'll only do it if you promise to let Ernie go free."

Captain Fangarm nodded. "That's a fair deal. I want to be eating squid by lunchtime, boy, so you'd better hurry up. Get off my ship!"

"And if you fail, we'll lock you both up for good!" Smullet added.

Albert's eyes darted to Ernie, whose face was ghostly white.

"Don't worry, Ern. I'll get you out of there," he called.

Smullet shoved him back up the steps. When they reached the top, a strange noise filled the air.

ooooOAAAHHHMMMMm!

A deep wailing sound, lasting about ten seconds.

"What was that?" asked Albert.

"Dunno," grunted Smullet. "We keep hearing it. Bloomin' annoying when you're trying to sleep. Now, don't let me see you again until this ship is back on water, else your friend's dead meat! You hear me?"

Albert nodded, trying to ignore the

panic rising through him.

With a final snarl, Smullet threw him out of the hole and back into the sheep field.

Chapter Five:
The Tentacle

Albert walked to the edge of the cliff and stared down. Waves gently lapped far below, but it felt like there was a storm spinning inside his head.

It's all my fault! he thought. *Ernie's trapped in the* Inkhunter *because of me. I have to get him out! But how can I get the ship back into the sea?*

oooooAAAHHHMMMMM!

It was the wailing sound again – and it was coming from the sea.

That sound must have something to do with what happened!

Albert had an idea.

He ran down the path to the beach and untied his boat. He jumped in and started rowing through the water.

oooooAAAHHHMMMMм!

There it was again, but louder. He was getting close.

Then he realised something: whatever

was making that sound was probably the same thing that made Rocco scream. Rowing towards it was not a good idea. But it was too late…

ooOOOAAAHHHMMMMM!

The noise came from under Albert's boat now, thundering through his ears. With shaking hands, he tried to turn the boat back towards the beach, but his oar hit something solid.

He looked over and saw a large, dark shape floating in the water.

ooOOOAAAHHHKKKKK!

The sound was different now – angry. Albert couldn't breathe. He gripped the oar tightly, and heard a splash in the water behind his boat.

Albert whipped round and saw something sink back into the sea. Something long and bright red.

"H-hello?" he stuttered. "Who – what are you?"

A shadow appeared over him. Albert stared up.

Hanging above the boat was a giant, red tentacle! At least a hundred times bigger than the boat, with many slimy, white suckers.

"Oh no!"

oooooAAAHHHMMMMm!

Albert pressed himself down flat against the bottom of his boat.

The tentacle waved menacingly in the sky above, then shot back into the sea. Albert's boat rocked wildly, then flew high up into the air.

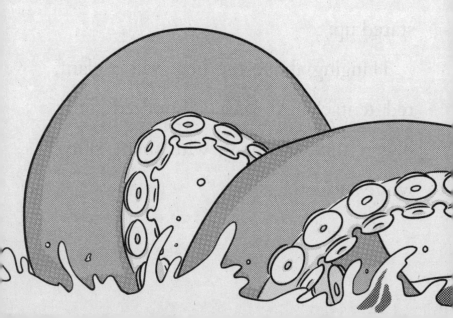

CHAPTER SIX:
Elody

"*AAAAAHHHHHHHHHHH!*"

He shut his eyes tight as the tentacle flung the boat through the air, higher than the cliff.

THUD!

Albert jolted forwards and tumbled

out of the boat, landing face first in something soft. He felt around him. Sand!

His boat had missed the cliff and landed on the beach under it. He sat up and spat sand out of his mouth.

So that's how the Inkhunter *got up onto the cliff!*

Albert looked out to sea. The giant red tentacle had disappeared, leaving just a few tall waves where it had been.

I can't have imagined it.

It must belong to a squid, but a giant one, hundreds of times bigger than the squid Rocco had in the glass bowl – a monster!

What made the giant squid so angry that it threw the Inkhunter *and my boat into the air?* Albert wondered.

If was impossible to understand what its cries meant. Unless…

Elody! Albert's mermaid friend! Mermaids were magical sea creatures like the squid must be. Elody might know why it was wailing.

"*If you want me to come and visit, or need my help again, talk into the silver shell and I will hear you,*" Elody had told him.

Albert dug into his pocket and pulled out the shell. He pressed it to his lips. "Elody, I need your help, quickly!"

All Albert could do was wait, so he sat

on the beach and worried about Ernie, trapped up with the pirates. Should he go and check if he was OK?

Just when Albert was about to give up and go back to the ship, a mass of curly black hair popped out of the sea right in front of him.

"Elody!" cried Albert.

"What's the matter, Albert?" asked Elody, bobbing up and down. "You sounded worried."

He walked to the edge of the water and explained everything that had happened to Ernie and him, and the *Inkhunter*.

OOOOOAAAHHHMMMMM!

Albert pointed out to sea. "That's the giant squid. Do you know what it's saying?"

Elody frowned. "I think I understand. But I need to get closer to hear it properly."

She disappeared under the water.

"Wait, Elody!" called Albert. "It's not safe. The squid is really angry!"

Her tail lifted up out of the water and,

with a flick, she was gone.

Albert bit his lip. Had he just sent Elody into danger?

Chapter Seven:
The Baby

Albert waited for several minutes with no sign of Elody. He pushed his boat back into the water. He had to find her – to save her from the giant squid!

A dark shape started to rise up next to his boat. The squid!

Albert grabbed an oar and jabbed it into the sea He lifted the oar above his head, ready to strike again…

The shape popped up out of the water.

"Elody!" Albert yelled.

Her eyebrows rose. "Albert!"

"Sorry! I thought the squid was attacking you."

"No, I was just talking with her," she replied with a giggle.

Albert's heart stopped racing quite as fast at the sight of her round, smiling face.

"She's the biggest squid I've ever met," said Elody. "In human language, her name is Shula."

"Did she say why she's angry?" Albert asked.

"Her baby, Numa, was stolen and she wants it back."

"Oh…" Albert thought about the pink tentacles in the glass bowl. "That must be the squid Rocco caught. No wonder Shula is angry!"

Elody nodded. "She tried to get Numa back, but in her panic she lost control of her tentacles and flung the ship up onto the cliff."

"Why doesn't she lift the *Inkhunter* back down again? Then she can rescue Numa."

"She's been trying, but her tentacles don't reach far enough up the cliff."

Albert leaned back to look all the way up at the *Inkhunter*.

"Rope…" he muttered.

"What do you mean?" asked Elody.

"I've got an idea. I'm going back up to the *Inkhunter*. Tell Shula to look out for rope. If she can pull the ship down, I'll make sure they give her baby back."

Chapter Eight:
Rope

Albert ran up to the *Inkhunter*. He really wanted to go inside and check that Ernie was OK. But he remembered what Smullet had said: *"don't let me see you again … else your friend's dead meat!"*

Albert had to do this without the pirates noticing.

He found steps carved into the side of the ship and climbed up to the deck. No one was there.

Albert searched around and found the ship's anchor lying on the deck.

Tied to it was what he was looking for: a long piece of rope. He dug his fingernails into the knot and unfastened the rope from the anchor. There was a sword on top of a barrel nearby. He used this to cut the rope in two.

Albert tied one piece of rope to the *Inkhunter*'s mainmast using a type of knot his granddad had taught him. He threw the rope over the side of the ship. It dangled halfway down the cliff.

He quickly did the same with the other piece, tying it to the foremast at the front of the ship.

Albert looked into the water and waved his arms for Elody and Shula to see. Far below a dark mass formed.

"ooooOAAAHHHMMMMM!"

Shula wailed.

A bright red tentacle burst out of the water. It rose up the cliff and Albert held his breath. Was the rope long enough? He let out a sigh of relief as the tentacle stretched up and clung to the very end, white suckers clamping around it. A second tentacle fired towards the other rope.

The *Inkhunter* jolted under Albert as Shula desperately pulled on both ropes. Albert tensed. The tentacles shook with effort.

"OOOAAAHHHFFF!"

With a roar, Shula's tentacles slipped off the ropes and flailed back into the water, sending waves crashing into the cliff.

"OOOOAAAHHHMMMM!"

Shula cried sadly.

She needs more rope! Albert realised.

He searched the deck, but couldn't see any more.

What else is long enough?

He looked around again, then up to the foremast. Of course! Attached to this was a huge white sail, flapping in the wind.

Albert grabbed the sword from the deck and, without stopping to think about it, climbed up the foremast's rigging until he was high above the *Inkhunter*. He felt like a tiny seabird, hovering above a great whale.

A strong breeze blew through him as

he tore the sail away from the mast with the sword. The bottom half came loose. He climbed further up the rigging and cut into the top half.

THHHHHUD!

The sail landed on the deck below. Albert froze, hoping the pirates hadn't heard. He waited for them to come storming onto the deck, but there was silence.

He climbed down the rigging as fast as he could and began

cutting the sail into long strips, using the sword to tear up the tough material.

Once he'd cut eight pieces, he tied them along the *Inkhunter*'s railings. They dangled down the cliff along with the two ropes.

"Try now, Shula!" Albert called.

Nothing happened. The water was flat and calm. Then…

"AAAHHH!"

Albert's vision filled with red. He jumped back. Not only did two tentacles fire out of the sea, but many other squid arms too. Each tentacle and arm grabbed hold of a rope or sail.

"Go on, Shula!"

"OOOOOAAAHHHFFFFF!"

A rumbling sound came from under Albert. His feet started to shake. The *Inkhunter* was moving!

Shula's tentacles and arms shook in her effort to pull it. Albert looked into her huge eyes, black and bulging. Her beak-like mouth opened wide with a cry.

"OOOOOAAAHHHFFFFF!"

"You can do it!"

The *Inkhunter* tipped forwards and Albert fell to the deck. He flung his arms around the mast as the ship swayed.

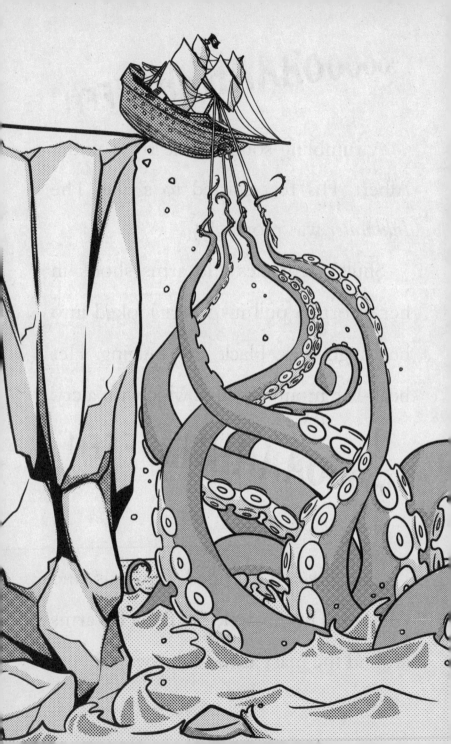

"OOOOOAAAHHHPPPP!"

The ship finally fell forwards. Albert's stomach lurched.

"Woaaaaah!"

It plummeted down the cliff, taking Albert with it. Wind rushed past him, burning his ears. Albert's feet rose into the air and he dug his fingers into the mast, only just clinging on as the *Inkhunter* soared downwards.

CRASH!

The ship landed in the water and rocked violently. A huge wave rose up over it, splashing down onto Albert.

Chapter Nine:
Attack!

Albert wiped the water from his face and blinked. A trap door burst open next to the *Inkhunter*'s wheel. Captain Fangarm climbed out, followed by the other pirates and, finally, Ernie.

"Ern!" Albert ran over and hugged his friend. "Are you OK?"

Ernie still looked pale, but nodded.

"Right, lads," said the captain. "Get your nets and rods ready. It's time to catch me some squid!"

The pirates headed off to different

parts of the ship.

"No!" cried Albert. "You have to give the baby back right now!"

Captain Fangarm frowned. "What baby?"

"oooooAAAHHHMMMMM!"

"Albert, quick – Shula is getting really worried!" he heard Elody call from the sea.

"The squid Rocco caught is called Numa," Albert explained. "You have to give it back to its mother, or else—"

"I told you, we can't get that squid off Rocco. That's why my men are catching more."

"Captain!" The cry came from the front of the ship.

Albert turned to see a pirate backing away from a giant red tentacle.

Captain Fangarm staggered back. Her eyes lit up. "Praise my left arm, that's *huge*!"

Then her eyes flashed black. Albert realised why. Rocco was walking towards the tentacle, holding the bowl up.

"That's why he was protecting the baby," said Ernie. "He wanted to give it back to its mother."

"Smullet, stop him!" Captain Fangarm growled. "That squid is mine. It should be in my belly. Get it off him!"

"YAAAAARRR!" Smullet charged towards Rocco and forced him to the ground. The bowl slipped along the deck and Smullet scooped it up.

"OOOOOAAAHHHKKKKK!"

Albert watched Shula's tentacle rise higher.

Captain Fangarm grabbed hold of the *Inkhunter*'s wheel and turned it. But she wasn't trying to avoid the tentacle – she was steering towards it!

Shula slammed her tentacle down, narrowly missing Smullet. Wood flew from the deck with a **CRUNCH!**

"Smullet, bring me the baby. The rest of you, fight that giant tentacle. The man who chops it off gets to choose how we cook it!" the captain ordered.

The pirates charged at the tentacle, swords raised. "Don't attack her!" cried Albert. "Just give her baby back."

"Silence!"

"OOOAAAHHHKKK!"

Albert turned to see
another tentacle rise up
on the other side of
the ship. It swept
three pirates off
their feet, and

the others charged at it. Thick black liquid fired out of the water.

Albert's eyes widened. *Squid ink!*

SPLAT! It hit the pirates right in their faces.

"*AAARGH!*" they yelled.

"Prepare the cannons!" Captain Fangarm barked.

Smullet was racing towards her with Numa. Albert had to stop him!

"Ern, can you get Captain Fangarm's attention?" he whispered.

Ernie frowned uncertainly, but nodded.

"C-captain," he stuttered, tugging her coat.

"What?!"

"Look – there's another tentacle behind you!" Ernie pointed.

Captain Fangarm followed his gaze. There was nothing there.

"It must have moved," said Ernie. "Look, over there!"

While the captain was turned away, Albert shot towards Smullet, halfway along the ship. The rest of the pirates were waving their swords at Shula's tentacles and loading a large cannon.

Albert didn't have time to worry. He grabbed the sword he'd used to cut the sail up and charged at Smullet.

Chapter Ten:
Fight!

BOOM!

The cannon fired.

Smullet stopped for a moment to watch the cannonball narrowly miss Shula.

This gave Albert just enough chance to catch up to him. Albert swung the sword, but the pirate was ready. He balanced the bowl in one hand, grabbed his sword with the other and knocked Albert back. A **CLANG** of metal on metal filled Albert's ears.

"Think you can fight me, boy?" Smullet snarled.

Albert gritted his teeth and swung his sword again. Smullet dodged sideways and swiped at Albert's head. Albert ducked just in time.

BOOM! The cannon fired again.

Albert saw Shula's tentacles disappear back into the water.

"oooooAAAHHHMMMMM!"

"Shula, over here!" Albert called.

"Shut it, boy!"
Smullet jabbed
his sword at Albert.
Albert blocked. The
force of the hit shook
his arm painfully.
As Smullet
swung

again and again, Albert saw Shula's tentacle rising up and moving towards Smullet. But the pirate didn't seem to notice it.

His eye patch! Albert realised. The tentacle was on Smullet's blind side.

With one eye on Shula, Albert kept blocking Smullet, trying to keep him in the same position so he couldn't see the approaching tentacle.

Just as the tentacle got to within touching distance, Captain Fangarm called, "Watch out, Smullet!"

The pirate looked around and his good eye boggled. He flung his sword at the tentacle. Albert tried to grab the bowl from Smullet's other hand, but he was holding it up too high.

Thick black ink fired out of the water. Albert ducked down as the ink hit Smullet with a **SPLAT!** He lost his balance, fell backwards and Numa flew out of the bowl and into the air.

Albert scrambled across the deck towards the baby squid, but a pirate caught it first. Albert tried to tackle him, but he tossed Numa to another pirate nearby.

"No!" Albert couldn't keep up as the baby squid was thrown from pirate to pirate, getting ever closer to Captain Fangarm.

"OOOAAAHHHKKK!"

A tentacle shot out of the sea again. The pirates stopped throwing Numa and watched the tentacle wrap around the *Inkhunter*'s mainmast and pull it.

SNAP! The mast split away from the ship. Albert jumped back as Shula dragged it along the deck, using it like a giant club to knock pirates out of the way.

"*AAAHHH!*" they screamed.

Albert pressed himself to the deck and the mast soared over him.

"Get up, men! Get up! Stop that tentacle!" Captain Fangarm yelped.

The mast hit the pirate holding Numa. He fell over a barrel, knocking the baby squid flying again.

It happened so quickly that Albert couldn't see where Numa had gone. He looked around and his heart stopped when he saw the baby squid clinging to one of Captain Fangarm's dreadlocks. The captain sniffed. Her eyes widened as she also realised where Numa was.

"NUMA!" Albert cried. "Ernie, do something!"

Ernie's eyes met with Albert's. "Your sword!" he called.

Albert threw the sword along the deck. It landed at Ernie's feet.

Captain Fangarm licked her lips and lifted her spike up to her dreadlock.

Ernie grabbed the sword. Albert hoped he was brave enough to fight the captain.

He raised the sword up and grimaced. Captain Fangarm's spike was centimetres from the baby squid.

Ernie swung the sword down. But not at Captain Fangarm exactly. At her dreadlock. It cut clean through, sending the hair and Numa falling to the deck.

Captain Fangarm frowned as her spike jabbed at thin air.

SPLAT!

"*AAARRRGGGHHH!*"

the captain yelled.

Squid ink landed on her head and glooped down her face.

Albert dodged around the other pirates, ran over and picked Numa up off the deck.

"OKKA! OKKA!" the baby cried.

"JUMP!" Albert called to Ernie.

Without looking back, they both flung themselves over the side of the ship and into the water.

Chapter Eleven:
Thank You

Albert and Ernie bobbed up and down in the sea, breathing deeply. A tentacle reached out of the water and gently took Numa from Albert's arm.

"ARRRAAALLL!

ASSSOOOEEE!"

"Shula says thank you," Elody explained, popping up and floating next to them.

Albert looked towards the ship.

Captain Fangarm staggered to the railings, wiping ink from her eyes.

"Give that squid back!" she snarled, baring her rotten teeth.

"OOORRRSSSTTT! KEGG!"

"Shula says that if she ever sees you pirates near Thistlewick again, she really will wreck your ship," said Elody.

Captain Fangarm turned to Smullet. They were both covered in ink from head to toe.

"Let's get out of here!" Smullet muttered.

"Unfurl the mainmast sail!" called the captain.

"Er, Captain," said one of the pirates. "That giant squid snapped the mainmast in two."

"Then unfurl the foremast sail!"

"Er … there's no sail on the foremast. Someone's ripped it off!"

"*AAARGH!*" If Captain Fangarm hadn't been covered in ink, she would be glowing red with anger now.

Albert, Ernie and Elody watched and laughed as the *Inkhunter* turned slowly around on the spot. It wouldn't get anywhere fast without its sails.

A bright red tentacle poked out of the

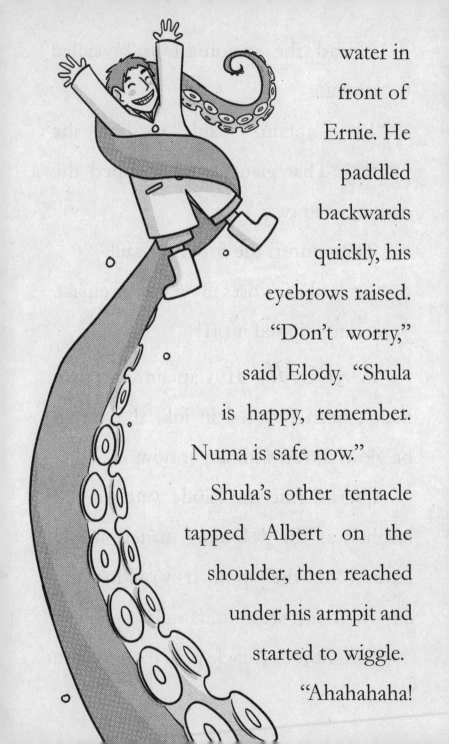

water in front of Ernie. He paddled backwards quickly, his eyebrows raised. "Don't worry," said Elody. "Shula is happy, remember. Numa is safe now." Shula's other tentacle tapped Albert on the shoulder, then reached under his armpit and started to wiggle. "Ahahahaha!

That tickles. Ahehehehe!"

The tentacle stopped tickling and hugged him softly. It felt squishy and warm.

"Can you take us back to my boat, Shula?"

"ARRRAA ALLL!"

Before Albert knew it, he was high up in the air. This time, though, he knew he was safe, wrapped in Shula's tentacle. Ernie rose up next to him and they high-fived.

They swung through the sky. Albert felt like he was a bird flying over the sea. He opened his arms out and pretended he had wings.

"WEEEEEEEE!"

His boat appeared below him on the beach and Shula gently placed him down next to it. Ernie landed nearby.

"Thank you, Shula," they called.

"ASSSOOOEEEEE!"

Her tentacles sucked back into the water, and she was gone.

Albert stared out to sea. Elody

disappeared under a wave, but a few seconds later, her head popped up next to the beach.

Albert smiled. "I thought you'd gone too. What were you doing?"

"I was inviting Shula to my birthday party next week. I will be 108!"

"Wow!" said Ernie.

"Can we come too?" asked Albert.

"Of course!"

Albert and Ernie shared a grin.

"So where's the shell, Albie?" Ernie asked. "You said I could look after it!"

"Here, Ernie," said Elody, as Albert was reaching into his pocket. She lifted a hand out of the water and opened it to reveal a small, silver shell. "This one's for you. You deserve it for saving Numa. Now you can both talk to me whenever you like."

Ernie took it and his eyes lit up. "As Shula would say, *ASSSOOOEEEEE!*"

A deep voice from the cliff above made them jump: "Ernie, where are you? I thought you were feeding the sheep."

"That's my dad," said Ernie. "We'd better go and see him."

Albert and Ernie waved goodbye to Elody and climbed to the top of the cliff.

Ernie's dad frowned at them. "Look at the two of you. You're both soaking wet! What have you been up to?"

Before they could answer, a sound came from the sea:

"ASSSOOOEEEEE!

ASSSOOOEEEEE!

ASSSOOOEEEEE!"

"And what on earth is that noise?" asked Ernie's dad. "It sounds like something crying."

"Oh, it's just the wind," said Albert.

He looked at Ernie and smiled again.

Only Albert, Ernie and Elody knew what Shula's cry really meant: "Thank you! Thank you! Thank you!"

AN iNterview With Albert aNd ErNie

INterVieWer: *Which was worse: the evil merpeople or the giant squid?*

ALBert: I was very scared of Shula when she first threw my boat up in the air. But she only did it because she was trying to get her baby back. The merpeople were definitely worse. They were just being horrible and trying to sink our boat for fun.

INterVieWer: *Ernie, what was is like being captured by the pirates?*

ErNie: Terrifying! When Captain Fangarm kept going on about how hungry she was, I thought she might try to eat me!

Interviewer: *How did you feel when baby Numa landed in Captain Fangarm's hair?*

Albert: It happened so quickly. I was shocked!

Ernie: Me too! I've never used a sword before, so I didn't know if I would be able to cut her dreadlock off. It was a scary moment.

Interviewer: *If you were a fish, what fish would you be?*

Albert: I'd be a swordfish. Then I'd be better at fighting against pirates!

Ernie: I'd like to be a clown fish.

Interviewer: *What are you getting Elody for her 108th birthday?*

Albert: Ernie came up with a really good idea for a present, but we're not going to tell you what it is. You'll have to wait to find out!

AN INTERVIEW WITH SHULA AND ELODY

INTERVIEWER: *Shula, how did you feel when the pirates took Numa from you?*

SHULA: OOOAAAHHH-KKKKK!

INTERVIEWER: *Elody, were you scared when you first spoke to Shula?*

ELODY: No. I've met giant squid before. I knew she was sad and wanted someone to talk to.

INTERVIEWER: *How many languages can you speak?*

ELODY: I can speak human, of course, and almost every underwater language. The only language I have trouble with is sea slug.

INTERVIEWER: *Did you think you, Albert and Ernie would be able to rescue Numa?*

ELODY: Oh yes. We make a good team! Albert seems to like getting himself into trouble, so I am sure we will have many more adventures.

SHULA: ARRRAAALLL!

INTERVIEWER: *What is your favourite word?*

ELODY: Sirenian.

SHULA: OPPYOPPYPOPPY!

AN INTERVIEW WITH THE SHEEP

INTERVIEWER: *Is it nice living on top of a cliff?*

SHEEP: Baah.

INTERVIEWER: *That's a very interesting answer. What did you think when the ship flew into your field?*

SHEEP: Baaaaaaaah!

INTERVIEWER: *Were you happy when the ship was no longer in your field?*

SHEEP: Bah baaaaah baaah.

AN INTERVIEW WITH Captain Fangarm

INTERVIEWER: *Captain Fangarm, what did you think when your ship landed on the cliff?*

FANGARM: I should have been worried about it, but I was too hungry to be worried! And I was annoyed that Rocco was keeping the squid to himself.

INTERVIEWER: *How did you feel when Albert and Ernie rescued the baby squid?*

FANGARM: I have never been more angry ... or more hungry!

INTERVIEWER: *What does your name mean?*

Fangarm: People think I am called Fangarm because I have a spike instead of a left hand. They are wrong! My father, the first great Captain Fangarm, was German. Fangarm is the German word for 'tentacle'. Maybe that is where my taste for squid comes from. Squid ... mmm ... tasty squid!

Interviewer: *If you were a fish, what fish would you be?*

Fangarm: The type of fish that eats squid!

Interviewer: *Thank you, Captain Fangarm.*

Fangarm: You said you'd give me a squid to eat if I answered your questions.

Interviewer: *Er ... sorry, I'm afraid I forgot to bring the squid.*

Fangarm: Grrrrr! Why you little—

Interviewer: *Wait! What are you doing? No! Please don't attack me with your spike! AAAAAAHHHHHHHHHH!!!*

ELOdy's GaMes

Work out the words from the clues
below and complete the puzzle.

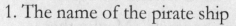

1. The name of the pirate ship
2. Albert's best friend
3. Captain _____ loves eating squid
4. The giant squid's baby
5. The pirate Albert fights with

How many times can you find the word SQUID written in the grid below? Look up, down, backwards and forwards!

S	Q	U	I	D	H	J	O
Y	R	M	P	O	S	G	A
S	W	D	I	U	Q	S	B
Q	C	I	F	Q	U	L	D
U	Z	U	T	S	I	R	I
I	O	Q	N	E	D	X	U
D	Z	S	K	V	G	B	Q
Y	P	W	D	I	U	Q	S

SQUID is written _____ times!

Luke Temple has written lots of other books, including:

The Blubber Monster's Crown

The Poo Monster

Albert and the Blubber Monster

Find out more about them at:

www.luketemple.co.uk